MARRA'S WORLD

MARRA'S WORLD
Elizabeth Coatsworth
Illustrated by Krystyna Turska

GREENWILLOW BOOKS
A Division of William Morrow & Company, Inc.
New York

Inquiries should be addressed to Greenwillow Books,
William Morrow and Company, Inc., 105 Madison Ave.,
New York, N.Y. 10016.
Printed in the United States of America.

1 2 3 4 5   79 78 77 76 75

Library of Congress Cataloging in Publication Data
Coatsworth, Elizabeth Jane (date) Marra's world.
Summary: Raised by a harsh grandmother and an
indifferent father, Marra comes to understand her
world with the help of her seal mother.
1. Turska, Krystyna (date)   II. Title.
PZ7.C629Mar   [Fic]   75-9520
ISBN 0-688-80007-6   ISBN 0-688-84007-8 lib. bdg.

For my contemporaries
whose friendship has lasted
through the years:
Helen, Agnes, Madeleine,
Louise, Bertha and Mary,
with much love always

Contents

MARRA'S WORLD

1. Marra

Marra's grandmother hated her and showed it every day of her life. She was a woman with a bad temper and Marra was afraid to be alone in the house with her. So far her grandmother had done nothing worse than scream at her, but once or twice Marra had seen her pick up the big kitchen knife and look at it thoughtfully in a way the child didn't like. As soon as

her father went off to his lobster boat, Marra
went too, off to the little beach at the back of
the island or, when it rained, to her shelter in
a grove of spruces, and there she stayed, play-
ing solitary games until the school bell rang.

After school it was the same thing again,
until her father's boat chugged into the small
harbor. She would have liked to have gone
home with one of the children in her class but
no one ever asked her to, and she did not dare
to invite them to her own house for fear of
what her grandmother might say or do.

Her father seemed to be on perfectly good—
or good enough—terms with the other men on
the pier, and her grandmother had one or
two old friends whom she occasionally went to
see. If one of them came to see her, she warned
Marra, "Don't you dare to come home until
dinnertime. I'm having company."

Her father, too, did not like Marra—she was sure of that. He never looked at her if he could help it. But she was not afraid of him. He occasionally gave her a little money to buy something at the store, and when he did this, she had an excuse to hang about Mr. Pratt's for a couple of hours, making her choice. This made the storekeeper nervous and he told her so, but Mr. Pratt was a kindly man and he didn't actually say that she had to get out, especially as it would usually be raining when she chose to do her ten cents' worth of shopping.

"You're worse than a deer fly for hanging around, Marra," he once told her between irritation and amusement.

"I have no place to go, Mr. Pratt," she said, and he shook his head.

"Well, you do no harm that I know of," he answered. "Stay if you have a mind to."

And half an hour later he gave her a bottle of Coke.

"But I've spent my money, Mr. Pratt," she cried, worried, for he had already taken off the top of the bottle.

He scowled at her.

"This is on the house," he said, turning away.

From that time on there grew up an almost silent, uneasy friendship between Mr. Pratt and Marra. She would slip into the store and begin putting it to rights. He was a somewhat untidy man and a busy one, as he was both postmaster and the only storekeeper on the island. His wife was dead and his son had gone to live on the Main. Marra found the broom behind the door and would sweep, as quietly as possible. If people came in, she would slip out of sight behind the shelves and stay out of

sight until they were gone. She also found the dustcloth and dusted. She piled the newspapers and magazines neatly. She even went so far as to arrange the cans on the shelves.

"I'm not paying you for any of this, Marra," Mr. Pratt warned her one day.

She looked up, with a quick smile. "It's enough just to be here, just to have something to do that I can do."

"Poor Marra," Mr. Pratt said. "Don't you help your grandmother at home?"

She shook her head. She never told anyone how things were at home.

After this Mr. Pratt talked more often with her and now and then he would give her something, an orange or an apple or a bar of candy. He spoke to her when she came in. She even thought that he liked to have her there.

For the first time in her life she felt that she belonged somewhere, not very securely, but still she had her place in the store. She had never made a place for herself in the one-room schoolhouse. The other children avoided her and the teacher spoke to her as seldom as possible. She was very slow at her lessons. Everything was harder for her to do than for the others. She was the last to learn to read and write and it seemed as if the multiplication tables were something she would never master.

"I don't know what's wrong with you!" Miss Nichols once exclaimed and the other children giggled, as if they knew but weren't telling. Marra didn't know. Everything about her life bewildered her.

2. Alison

*I*t was on a day of heavy fog that life changed for Marra. Everything began as usual, waking up in her little room under the roof to hear her father's boots on the stairs, the silent breakfast with Granny handing her food as if she hoped it would choke her. Pa and Granny spoke a few words together. "Burn off?" asked Granny.

"Ayeh," said her father. "About eleven."

Marra looked up. She said nothing, but Pa asked (which was an unusual thing for him to do), "What do you think, Marra?"

"I think it will hang around here all day," she said hesitantly.

Lately he had begun to notice that she could predict weather better than the weather bureau or he himself for that matter.

"Maybe so," said Pa.

Granny didn't like that.

"A lot she knows," she muttered to herself.

"I'll do some work in the garden," her father said.

"It will clear," said Granny in her laying-down-the-law voice. "No need to hang around the place, Ken."

"Another cup of coffee," said her father.

Marra, greatly daring, started to get up to get it for him, but Granny's voice jerked her back to her seat.

"I'll do that!" she said. "You're likely to spill the pot if the handle's a little hot."

That was something which had happened a long time ago, when Marra was quite a little girl, but Granny never forgot anything Marra had ever done badly. She never showed her how to do anything about the house, nor even taught her how to work in the garden.

"I'd rather do it myself," she said grimly to her son. "That child doesn't know a weed from a flower. I came in the other day and there she was pumping water to fill a tumbler—to put dandelions in! What can a person do?"

Pa shrugged. The easiest thing was to ask

nothing of Marra. What could be expected of a child like that?

Marra got up and pulled an old coat from the hook behind the door, and went out. She had no manners. She had never been taught any, except a few at school by an annoyed teacher. She knew enough to close the door quietly, and then she entered her world.

The fog was so thick it seemed almost like whitened water in which only the nearest objects could be made out. It was cool and clinging, it seemed to open about Marra as she walked and close about her when she had passed. Every bush and tree was dripping. A faint light, neither that of sun nor moon, brightened on the drops of moisture hanging from every leaf and grass blade. Not a breath of air stirred, and there was not a sound except for the tap, tap of the dewdrops and the far-off and mournful blat of the foghorn.

Marra's rough coat was soon silvered with the fog, and her hair clung to her cheeks, and she was smiling to herself. This was the weather that she loved; it was on such a day that she became beautiful, though no one ever noticed it and such a thought would not have occurred to her as being possible.

But on this particular morning, someone did notice it. When the school bell rang and she dragged herself away from the nearby beach to the barren schoolyard and the even more barren school, there was a new girl in the usually empty seat beside Marra's. Her name was Alison Dunbar and she had blue eyes and an eager face.

"You're wet through," she whispered to

Marra. "You'll catch your death of cold."

"It won't hurt me," Marra whispered back. "I don't mind being wet."

She knew that the girl was the daughter of the new doctor who had come just last week to the harbor, for on an island everything is known even to such an isolated soul as Marra. They had taken the old Gildersleeve house.

"You're the first person I ever knew who was pretty when her hair was wet," Alison whispered in the stir between classes.

"Me—pretty?" Marra said out loud in her astonishment, and several of the nearest children who overheard her laughed.

"Marra's pretty! Marra's pretty!" they chanted in derision.

They saw her as she was—a thin little girl in a cheap dress several sizes too large for her,

her big brown eyes always bewildered and her motions fumbling.

"Well, I never!" exclaimed Tessy Jewett, whose father dealt in lobsters. "Marra pretty! Will wonders never cease?"

"Hush, children," said Miss Nichols. "Let's see how well you've studied your geography lesson."

She was not surprised to find that Marra had either not studied it at all or had learned nothing if she had.

Miss Nichols really looked at the child this morning, wondering if it could be true that she was pretty. She seemed only lank, ill-dressed and stupid to Miss Nichols, as she had always seemed, a little more so for being so damp. What had made the new girl say a thing like that? She might have been teasing. The children teased Marra a lot, which on the whole seemed only natural to Miss Nichols, who, however, always told them to stop if she heard them. But she usually had something better to think about.

3. At the Doctor's House

*T*hat was the beginning of the curious, lop-sided friendship between Alison and Marra. All the advances were on Alison's side. Marra hung back or occasionally responded with an almost desperate gratitude. But she had something to give Alison in return for her friendship—the island itself which she knew as none of the other children bothered to know it. She

knew where the fiddlehead ferns grew or the terns nested. She knew where the little beaches lay between the rocky points and as the final gift of her affection she showed Alison the small cave hidden beyond the boulders on Cary's Point. It would hold only one child at a time but it *was* a cave, a real cave, and Alison left a penny there so that they might call it the Treasure Cave. Marra showed her the woods where the herons nested and the ruins of the old shipyard where fishing boats had been built.

"I think my great-grandfather owned it," she said.

"Don't you know?" asked Alison. "Why don't you ask your father?"

Marra didn't answer. She didn't tell Alison that she never asked Pa anything, not since she had asked him about her mother long ago.

"Did she die?" she had asked Pa once when they were alone on his fish pier.

"She went away," he had answered after a long silence. "Don't talk about her. She'd have made no sort of a mother to you, anyway. She was dumb."

"Maybe that's why I'm so stupid," said Marra.

"I didn't say she was stupid. I don't know about that. She didn't talk. Most of the time, she was dumb like a deaf and dumb person."

He had glowered at the net he was mending and as Marra didn't say anything, at last he said, "She could only speak once in a while for a day or two. She didn't know how to do anything about the house either, and Granny wouldn't show her. I don't blame Granny. It wasn't easy for her. Sometimes I've thought it was her who drove Nerea away."

"Didn't you want her to go?" Marra had dared to ask. It was the first and only time she had ever talked with her father, but at this one time and place they did talk.

He had three more words to say before he became silent forever—about anything that mattered—and that was when, after another long silence, he had said slowly and sadly, "No, I didn't."

Then he had burst out in his usual rough tone, "Don't ever speak of her again to me or to anyone else. And stop hanging around! I have my work to do."

Marra had gone away. She had always wished that she had a mother, but now her mother had become a mystery to her, a mother who didn't talk, a mother who was no good at housework, a mother whom Granny hated and whom her father—unwillingly perhaps— missed. Could she have been a foreigner per- haps, shipwrecked on the island? She often thought about her, dreamed about her even, but she never dared ask about her. Sometimes she wondered if it could have been because of her mother that the children at school wouldn't play with her. Could she ask Mr. Pratt? But Pa had told her not to talk about her mother to anyone and she was afraid to, anyway, afraid of what she might learn.

But Alison, too, came from a different world, from the Main, and Alison was her friend. The other children at first would have been glad to make friends with Alison, for she was the doctor's girl, but when from the beginning she chose out Marra for her especial friend, they began to treat her somewhat as they did Marra, as someone whom they couldn't see or hear. Alison only laughed.

"I can get along without them," she told Marra. "Mother wants you to come for lunch with us today. I hope your granny won't mind."

Granny just said, "Good riddance!" when Marra ran up to the kitchen door to ask her. But as Marra ran off again Granny looked after her with curiosity and then glanced sharply at the doctor's daughter who was waiting for her beyond the apple tree.

Looks all right, thought Granny, but she must be crazy to want Marra. The child doesn't know a fork from a spoon.

She would have been surprised to see how

carefully Marra hid her ignorance of the behavior proper at table. Her big brown eyes watched and copied every move of the doctor and his wife. She did nothing that they did not do and showed no sign that some of the food she had never tasted before. She spoke only when spoken to and sat as Alison sat and excused herself before the coffee was brought in, as Alison did.

"What a pretty child, no, a beautiful child," said the doctor when the girls had run off to school.

"Yes, beautiful," said his wife. "But her beauty has a sort of strangeness about it, don't you think?"

"All beauty has a strangeness about it," said the doctor. "She does look too pale, as if she doesn't get enough to eat. And where on earth do those clothes come from?"

4. The New Marra

*T*he doctor's wife began remaking Marra along with her clothes.

"They're too big for you," she told Marra.

"Yes," agreed Marra. "Granny orders them from the mail-order house for me to grow into, but by the time they fit me they're so old they have to be used for cleaning rags."

"How many dresses have you?" asked Mrs. Dunbar.

"Two," said Marra. "One to wash and one to wear."

"But you could turn up the hems, couldn't you?"

"I don't know how to sew." Marra was shamefaced. "Granny says I can't do anything, but I do redd up Mr. Pratt's store. I could redd up the house, too, if she'd let me. But she doesn't want me underfoot."

The doctor's wife's mouth tightened. "I'll drop in to talk to your grandmother next time I go by."

After that talk she understood a little more what Marra was up against. "She's an old she-devil!" she said to her husband in private. "But she did say I might take up hems and put in wider seams in those horrible dresses of Marra's, so long as I didn't cut any of the cloth.

She didn't want to allow even that, but she couldn't think how to refuse."

"That means extra work for you," said the doctor.

"It won't take long on my sewing machine. Anyway, I do want to see what the child looks like when she's not dressed like a scarecrow. And she's Alison's friend."

So first one dress was shortened and fitted and then the other. Marra was as delighted as Alison and her mother by the results. Mrs. Dunbar put some embroidery on the second dress, which was of an unpatterned material.

"I can't believe it's me!" said Marra. "Oh! Thank you, thank you!"

Mr. Pratt complimented her on how well she was looking when she dropped in to redd up the store as she did almost every day. Without the humiliation of the oversized dresses Marra changed. She carried herself better and smiled more often. The children in school noticed. It wasn't as easy to make fun of this Marra, and some of them began to speak to her as if she were just another girl in the class. Oh, they weren't friendly. They were neutral, waiting to see what happened next.

What happened next was that Alison's mother made Marra a dress of soft red wool for Christmas, with a white collar and cuffs. "You'll have to take them off and wash and iron them and put them back," she warned her. "But you can do it over here while Alison is changing hers. It won't take you long to learn."

And that was how Marra learned to wash and iron and sew under Mrs. Dunbar's kind

eye. At first she was all thumbs, and like school work, it never came easily to her, but she did learn. Mr. Pratt began to pay her a little for her work at the store, although she protested that she liked to do it. With the money she bought a pair of shoes, making out the order with the help of Alison and her mother. When she wore the red dress and her new shoes it was almost too much for the school.

"Mory, Mory,
In all her glory!"

they chanted, but she didn't care. She knew that she looked nice and that they thought so, too. She did better with her schoolwork, but even so, not very well. She was aware of every bird and beast, of every tree and flower, of the ways of the sea and of the clouds and wind, but addition and subtraction remained things that she could learn only as a parrot learns. In time she could recite the multiplication tables without a mistake, but still she had no clear idea of how to add or subtract, let alone to multiply.

"It's not as though you were really stupid, Marra," Miss Nichols told her in one of their many after-school sessions. "But you get the lowest grades."

"The things I know about aren't in books, Miss Nichols," Marra said, twisting uncomfortably in her chair. "I try. I try very hard and Alison tries to help me. Sometimes I think maybe I'm beginning to understand figuring, but when I try to do it by myself, I have no idea what it's about."

"You understand well enough what you

should get for change when you give Mr. Pratt a quarter for a bar of candy."

"No, I don't even understand that. I take what he gives me, Miss Nichols. I'm just plumb stupid, I guess."

But Alison thought she was clever. On their walks Marra saw, heard and smelled twice as many things as Alison did, and knew what they were and what they meant.

"It's fascinating," Alison told her mother. "It's as though Marra lived in a different world from the rest of us, a beautiful, scary, secret world."

The doctor's wife took this with a grain of salt.

She laughed. "Don't go and get lost in Marra's world," she said.

5. The Picnic.

*I*n March there came a day like May, a Saturday, too.

"I'll put up a picnic for us and we'll go somewhere—oh, somewhere where we've never been before," said Alison.

By now she understood that Marra didn't dare ask to take any food out of her house. Her grandmother didn't hold with such goings on.

She didn't want Marra around, but she had no intention of helping her to even the simplest sort of happiness elsewhere. All this foolishness Mrs. Dunbar was putting into the child's head! Everything must be just so, her dresses all prettied up, the good money she earned spent for new shoes, instead of being used to help pay for the food she ate. She was even asking for second helpings these days, and her father, like a fool, abetted her, now that she was going about all gussied up with her head in the air. Well, you can't make a silk purse out of a sow's ear, she always said.

So on this March-May morning the girls started off with their picnic basket which Mrs. Dunbar had put up for them. After that one visit with Marra's grandmother, she had a pretty good idea why Marra's life was different from that of any of the other children, and she did her best to make up to her for the harshness with which she lived day in, day out.

"Let's go some place new," suggested Alison again. "We've never been to the east end of the island."

"I'm not supposed to go there, ever."

"Is it dangerous?" asked Alison.

"I think there are cliffs, maybe."

"We can keep well back from the edge, if there are," argued Alison. "Oh, do come along! Let's have a real adventure. Probably your father told you not to go there when you were little and might have fallen off. You're big now."

"Not very big," said Marra laughing, for she was small for her age. "And I'm still clumsy. But I don't think I'd fall over a cliff. Pa'd

probably let me go now—with you, anyway."

She wanted to go very much. Always the east
end of the island had been what attracted her
most. She didn't know why because she had
never been there. But sometimes she dreamed
about it at night and in her dream she would
think that she stood on a black cliff and that
something very wonderful was just about to
happen. Then she would wake up and sometimes she would hear the wild, unearthly call
of a loon flying overhead. Had that been what
wakened her, she would wonder. She didn't
think so. It had been some more mysterious
thing that had been about to happen in her
dream, too wonderful to be disclosed perhaps.

So on this March-May day filled with flying

sunlight and a breeze that was soft and smelled of the sea, she decided that Alison must be right. Pa hadn't meant that she was never to go to the end of the island, only that she wasn't to go there when she was little. In her heart she knew that he had meant "Never at all," but she was beginning to rebel against her family which gave her orders in plenty, but never love.

"It's my turn to carry the basket," she said. "I know Granny calls me 'butter fingers,' but I won't drop it."

There was a clear path heading eastward, and once beyond the last houses, it began to climb. There were a few spruces but not many. Mostly the ground was covered with turf and angelica and boulders. Several cows were feeding there, one of them with a calf. It was

curious and friendly and walked toward the girls, but its mother called it back.

"She's telling it we're no-good islanders and she wouldn't trust us with so much as a herring," said Marra laughing.

At last after quite a climb they came to the top of a cliff as Marra had guessed. But she hadn't guessed how black it would be, with a white beach between its paws. The girls sat down with the picnic basket between them, looking out toward the horizon. The sea was dappled with small whitecaps restless as a flock of birds. They broke on the beach below in mimic fury. On that warm day everything seemed to be gay. The gulls and terns weren't still for a moment. The clouds were chasing one another, and so were their shadows on the sea, and the little waves were as sportive as they. The sound that they made in breaking along the sand was not loud, but a louder reverberation seemed to come from the headland that lay below them to the right.

"There must be a cave there," said Marra, "I wish we could see it."

"No," said Alison. "Remember what your father said. It was probably the cave he had in mind. The path down to the beach is very scary and goodness knows how we could get into the cave. We'd get soaked at the very least."

And then it was that they heard the singing.

6. The Singing

The singing had no words. It was almost like a natural sound, like a wind among birch trees or ripples in a cavern, or more still, like a bird singing in early spring. Yet none of these sounds would have had the tenderness and sadness of this singing. Alison felt it and listened to it, motionless and almost afraid, it was so beautiful and so unlike anything else. But

Marra listened as if her heart were listening. This singing spoke to her of forgotten emotions, of memories beyond the reach of her memory, of feelings she might once have had but which the years had buried deeply away. After a little while, unconsciously, she too began to sing. The song from above the cliff and the one from below were often blended into one song and sometimes separated and then were joined again. The tears were running down Marra's face as she sang, and when the unseen singer ended her song on a note of almost unbearable sweetness, Marra flung herself on the ground and began to cry in great silent sobs.

Alison bent over and put her hand on Marra's shoulder.

"It's all right, it's all right, Marra," she soothed her. "It must have been all right, it was so beautiful."

Marra sat up, drying her eyes. "Of course it's all right," she said. "I don't know why I was so upset. I felt, well I felt—"

"You felt?"

"I felt as if everything that's been wrong with me was right now. It didn't matter about school grades, or Granny's scolding. Something understood all that, understood how hard I try, understood and well—loved me. Did you feel that?"

"No, I just felt that it was beautiful and mysterious."

Alison thought that Marra had a different look, a glowing look that she had never noticed before. Her eyes seemed so large and filled with an inner shine, perhaps from unshed tears. Her long hair was ruffled, but it appeared to fall in waves, and her mouth seemed redder and more beautiful.

Alison shook herself. Marra's the same. It's just me. That singing has made me romantic about things. And it was true. Sky and sea and cliffs seemed to embrace the girls lovingly as they sat side by side on the black headland with the picnic basket between them.

Alison turned eagerly to Marra. "Sing again and see if it will answer you."

Marra shook her head.

"No, we have to wait until it's ready."

"Maybe it will never be ready again."

"We've had this. You can't expect miracles every ten minutes. Whatever happens, we've had this."

The picnic finished, they walked back very soberly to the village, saying little.

Once Alison said, "It was for you. I just happened to be there."

Marra thought for a while. "I think it was for us both, but more for me perhaps, because I've been so unhappy for so long."

And later she said, "We mustn't tell anybody."

"Of course not!" cried Alison. "I have some sense! Nobody who hadn't been there would understand it anyway."

7. The Window

Marra slept in a little bare room in the attic. A cot, a chair and a bureau with drawers that stuck when she tried to open them were its only furnishings. Oh yes. There was an old rag rug on the floor and that winter Pa had brought up from the cellar a small rusty stove and fitted it into the chimney.

"She doesn't need that any more than a cat

needs two tails," said Granny. "All she has to
do is to keep her door open and the warmth
from the rest of the house will keep her room
above freezing."

"Not much above," Marra had overheard
Pa say. "If you think we haven't enough wood,
Marra can get her own wood from the beach.
But mind, what she gathers is hers. Don't
swipe it. I keep plenty piled beside your stove
always!"

In spite of this warning, Granny did levy
tribute on Marra's wood, but not for long. Her
Pa cut spruce from their woods for the stoves.
He at once recognized the driftwood that
Granny tried to conceal under it.

"I told you," he said more sternly than he
usually spoke to Granny, "to let the child have
her wood in peace. And see to it that you serve

her larger helpings at meals. The doctor stopped me to say that she's undernourished."

"Fiddlesticks!" said Granny. "Let him mind his own business. She gets plenty."

But now under her son's eye she was more generous with the servings that she gave Marra. Mrs. Dunbar had made the girl another soft wool dress, blue this time, which Marra loved even better than the red one. It was hard for Granny to treat this well-dressed child like a stray cat as she had in the old days. She felt no love for her, but the old contempt had softened.

Some ways she takes after my family, she thought. I never supposed she'd be able to do as much about the house as she does. Likely she copies what she sees me do.

In her heart of hearts she knew well enough

that she always shooed Marra out of any room where she was working.

"Out you go!" she'd say. "You make me nervous."

What Marra had learned, she learned from Mrs. Dunbar, to whom she had become almost like another daughter. At school both Miss Nichols and the other children were aware of the change in her. Still the girls didn't invite her to their houses, but they included her in the games they played in the schoolyard and they no longer whispered and giggled about her.

As for Miss Nichols, she had given up trying to teach Marra what she couldn't seem to learn. She didn't give her arithmetic homework or call on her to go to the blackboard to do sums. She let her just sit through the class quietly dreaming.

As Marra began to write more easily, Miss Nichols found that she often wrote poetry, and it was better poetry than Miss Nichols realized, but even she gave her A's on her papers. In geography Marra was slow, but she never forgot what she learned and in natural history she was at the head of the class.

"We just have to take her as we find her," Miss Nichols told the school board when the subject came up. "She'll never graduate, but there are some things she's good at. It would be of no use to put her in a lower grade."

The school board hemmed and hawed but gave in, so long as it was understood that Marra would never graduate.

"She's a little feeble-minded," said one of them, "which is queer when she's got a smart father and grandmother."

"She must take after her mother's family,"

said another. "Do you remember her? She was dumb."

"Yes, and very beautiful."

"Marra is getting to be beautiful, too, and she's queer, but I don't think she's feeble-minded."

So the opinion of the village rested, less set than it had been. The friendship of Dr. Dunbar's family and of Mr. Pratt made a wide breach in the solid circle of disdain in which Marra had once lived.

Other than the cot, the chair, the bureau whose drawers always stuck, the old rag rug and the little stove with driftwood beside it, there was one more thing in Marra's room.

There was the dormer window facing east, and one spring night Marra was awakened by the light of the full moon falling through it

across her pillow and full on her face.

Immediately she was wide awake. She got up and dressed silently. Once she thought, What am I getting dressed for in the middle of the night? But very strongly from deep in her came the answer, You must go, and go quickly.

She carried her old shoes in her hand as she tiptoed down the stairs, and for once the creaking stairs were silent and when she had put on her coat, the door opened silently as she went out. It was as though they were in a conspiracy with her and were helping as best they could.

Shall I ask Alison to go with me? she thought as she ran eastward along the path, but something answered, No, not this once.

8. The Islands

*L*ater she could remember clearly running out of the dark house into the bright white light of the full moon. She had gone to East Point, she thought, for there had been the shadowy spruces, and she thought that she had heard voices singing, not one this time, but many. When she came to the end of the point, there seemed to be figures dancing on the

beach, or had she just dreamed that? For later she was quite sure she had seen seals frolicking in the waves. And someone had talked to her, someone named Nerea who was her mother. She had been swept by happiness. "Can't I stay with you?" she thought she had begged, but her mother had answered sadly, "No, you have to be born a seal to live with the seals."

At least it seemed to Marra that her mother had said that. But like the dreams she had often had about the cliff, the memory became vaguer and vaguer the next morning as she dressed. When she reached the kitchen she could not even remember the beautiful name "Nerea." The real people were Granny who was standing by the stove giving her a scowl and saying, "You're late. Hurry now," and her father who nodded and said, "Hi!" They were the solid facts in the life she knew. Songs and dances and seals, all that night enchantment under the full moon were things as insubstantial as dew. For a very little while she was glad that she had even imagined them, but by the time she had reached the hubbub of the schoolyard and waved to Alison, the memory had grown so faint that she could find no words for it. And then it was gone altogether.

But she was changed. Something of the assurance of being loved by Nerea had entered into her even if Nerea was forgotten. Now she accepted herself as she was and before long other people began to accept her, too, Alison and her family first of all, then Mr. Pratt, then Miss Nichols and the children at school, then Pa and last of all Granny who nagged at her less and less and one day, in an absent-minded moment, praised her for something.

"There, considering who you are, you don't do too badly."

One day during the summer vacation Alison and Marra were at loose ends. They had finished their chores and had no particular plans. It was Alison who suggested a picnic on the Cow and Calves, three small islands not more than forty minutes' row from the harbor. There were usually sheep on Cow Island and they thought there was a ram on Big Calf. They'd see when they got there. There was a small beach on Little Calf which might be best of all. It was scarcely more than a rock where the terns nested, but there were the ruins of the hermit's cabin to give it a sense of strangeness. No one quite knew who the hermit was or how long ago he had built his shelter or when he had died. There were just two walls of beach stones still standing under a single spruce tree. Most people thought he had been a pirate, so now and then the boys went out and dug for treasure, but no one had ever found a sign of it.

"What I wonder about was where he got his drinking water," someone would say.

"He could have had a catchment at the foot of that cliff," another would suggest, "or there may have been a little spring which has dried up since his time. I've known that to happen."

So there was something rather special about Little Calf even if you didn't believe in ghosts, and the girls told each other that they weren't scared of any old ghost.

"It's never done anyone any harm," said Alison. "It won't hurt us even if there is such a thing."

"No, I don't suppose so, but it is true that people have heard queer noises, and when Jerry Sinclair had been digging there a northeaster came up all of a sudden on the way back and nearly swamped his dory," said Marra.

"Well, we shan't dig." Alison was set on the picnic. The day was mild, with no wind or almost none. "Mother will let us make sandwiches. Why are you hanging back, Marra?"

It was true that Marra didn't feel very eager for the adventure, but she didn't know why. She had often longed to explore the islands but she didn't like to ask Pa to lend her his tender which he left tied up to his float when he took the lobster boat out. Now they would use the doctor's light new rowboat which was waiting at the pier. She didn't even have to ask Granny, who never cared where she was after the work which she nowadays did was finished.

"Scat!" Granny would say when the last chore had been done. "And don't let me see hide nor hair of you until the boats are in."

Granny didn't speak as fiercely as she used to. Sometimes her harshness seemed to be more from habit than from feeling, and Marra had been told by one or two of Granny's friends that Granny even said, "Some ways she's a little like my Aunt Lola."

She didn't say that to Marra and Marra knew better than to expect any kind word from her, but there was a general easing of the tension in the house. The fierce edge of Granny's hatred had worn down to dislike and even to tolerance. Still, Marra asked no favors from Granny and knew she would get none if she asked. But Alison was welcome to use her father's rowboat any time she wanted to, and they would put up the picnic at Alison's.

Still Marra hung back.

Something in her warned her, Don't go today, but she didn't know why. Not today, said her inner self, but outwardly it seemed exactly the right day. Pa had said that morning, "Should have a good day today. All signs point to it." But some sign in Marra didn't point to a good day. Yet here it was nearly noon and it was as fine as it had been at dawn.

"All right," said Marra, still a little hesitantly. "I've always wanted to explore Little Calf, and if we stay late we can come home by moonlight. Moon's at the full tonight."

9. Nerea

*T*hey never reached the three islands. Marra rowed and Alison sat in the stern and handled the tiller. There was no sea running, just enough to bring the little wavelets to flower, and the flock of terns that seemed to follow them for a while seemed like flowers, too, against the sky, or so Marra thought, but Alison only laughed at her.

"We're getting very near," said Alison.

"Don't you want me to take the oars for a while? I'm not as good at rowing as you are, but you must be getting tired."

"I'm fine," said Marra, resting for a minute to turn her head and look at the islands they were approaching. There was Cow Island with a cliff and sheep feeding on the short turf, and Big Calf, where the ram was probably exiled, and Little Calf circled by reefs. She even noticed the ruin of the pirate's house and some stones by the shore piled for a landing long ago. A glance showed her all this, but what her gaze steadied on was the sun. Surely it was not as bright as it should have been?

"Alison, isn't it cooler than it was?"

"Yes," said Alison comfortably. "It was too hot when we started out. Marra, what on earth are you doing?"

"I'm heading the boat for home," said

Marra. "Help me, Alison. The fog is coming in. Look hard at our landing and try to steer for it even when you can't see it. The trouble is that everyone naturally rows harder with the right oar than with the left, and a boat like this can be turned completely in the wrong direction in a fog without either of us knowing."

"But I can see our landing perfectly well."

"Now, you can," said Marra. "I hope you still can in ten minutes," and she began to row at a fast, steady pace. She had grown up hearing stories of dories and lobster boats, too, in heavy fogs carried out to sea by the tides. Some had been lost for days and some forever.

"You're making a lot out of nothing," said Alison uneasily.

"I hope so," said Marra. Alison was an inland girl. She might know the dangers of bliz-

zards but she knew nothing of fogs nor of the treachery of tides nor of their strength when the moon was full.

Marra went on rowing. Her back was to their destination, but already Cow Island and the Calves were blotted out by a thin veil of fog.

"I can still see the landing," said Alison. Her voice trembled a little, but she tried to hold it steady. Marra's fear had been communicated to her, Marra's courage, too, but she had plenty of her own.

It was almost as if the fog had heard her for now neither she, nor Marra, when she turned her head briefly to verify her position, could see the landing on their own island nor its dwelling houses and trees and the fringe of fish houses and piers below them. The white moist presence of the fog drifted all about them, turning the sun into something like a small frantic moon and then wiping it out altogether. Now they moved through nothingness. Even sounds were distorted. Somewhere far off a dog barked, a small familiar sound, but they could not tell whether it was ahead of them or to one side.

"Don't row too hard with your right oar," said Alison.

"I'm trying not to," said Marra. "Try to sit just as you were sitting before we lost sight of the landing place."

"I can't be sure!" wailed Alison.

There was a long, long silence while they moved through the dense white cocoon of the fog, and at last Alison said, "Marra, shouldn't we have reached the landing by now?"

"I think so," said Marra. "I suppose we're going to land in Spain, and won't the Spaniards be surprised?"

If she had hoped to make Alison laugh, she succeeded. Alison gave a little snort of amusement and then, having once opened the door of her silence, burst into tears.

"Don't cry, Alison, don't cry. We may meet a lobster boat or something."

She was much more upset for Alison than for herself. Many people would miss Alison, but no one would miss her, or at least only a little. She didn't think about that, only felt her heart filled with a longing to protect Alison, her first friend. And with the sharpness of that emotion a forgotten memory awoke. The spell which had been laid over the memory of Nerea thinned and now it was gone.

"Nerea!" she shouted. "Nerea! Nerea! Help us, Nerea!"

And almost at once, close beside them Nerea appeared, a gray seal this time with kind, mournful eyes. She nudged against the bow of the boat, turning it. "Don't try to steer, Alison," said Marra. "It will be easier for Nerea if you let her do it all."

The seal gave her a backward look, wise and loving.

"Oh, Nerea, we are so glad that you came!" Marra sighed. She went on rowing, slowly, so as not to interfere with the seal's movements. Then, as the specter of the pier loomed more than life-sized out of the fog, Nerea gave Marra one long, last loving look and disappeared, taking all memory of herself and the rescue with her.

"Thank you," Marra began, but then forgot whom she was thanking. "Thank you, Alison, for steering us so well."

"I don't think I steered well," said Alison uncertainly, but she, too, had forgotten who or what it was that had brought them home. With stiff hands they fastened the painter of the boat to the float and climbed up its short, slippery ladder.

Only when on the pier they almost bumped into the small bent figure in a man's reefer did they recognize Marra's granny. But she saw them before they saw her.

"Only a couple of fools wouldn't have known that a fog was coming in," she told them crossly. "The others think you're off in the woods for your picnic. But I knew better. I watched where you were off to from the kitchen window. Now come on up to the house! Come on, Alison, you too. I've got hot chocolate on the stove and fresh beaten biscuits in the oven waiting for you. No use wasting them, now you're here."

Marra was too surprised to answer, but Alison said at once, "Thank you, Granny. We're half frozen."

The full moon is the key
It opens the gates of night
It makes the dog howl
and the tides rise high on their beaches.
Shadows change
Breezes are aware
Owls move silently on feather-soft wings
Now is the moment when the powers of magic
Are at their strongest.
Pull down the shades of the house
Close the doors
Even the stars draw back
It is the hour of the full moon
And nothing is certain.

$\mathcal{E}$LIZABETH COATSWORTH is considered one of the truly distinguished writers for children in this century. In 1931 she received the Newbery Medal for *The Cat Who Went to Heaven*. She was also honored as first runner-up for the Hans Christian Andersen Award in 1968, the only international award given for an author's complete work.

Miss Coatsworth lives in Nobleboro, Maine. Among her recent books are *All-of-a-Sudden Susan*, *Pure Magic,* and a revised edition of her first book, *The Cat and the Captain.*

$\mathcal{K}$RYSTYNA TURSKA was awarded the 1972 Kate Greenaway Medal for the best picture book published that year in Great Britain, *The Woodcutter's Duck*. Reviewers on both sides of the Atlantic were united in their admiration of it; and it was also a 1973 Book World Spring Festival Honor Book. She has written and illustrated several other favorite picture books, including *The Magician of Cracow.*